Tell Me
what it's like to be
BIG

Joyce Dunbar

Illustrated by Debi Gliori

DOUBLEDAY

London · New York · Toronto · Sydney · Auckland

Morning peeped through the window.
Willa was first to wake up.

She put on her jumpsuit
this way...
and that way...
until it was right.

Then Willa put on
her chicken slippers
and went downstairs
to have breakfast.

No-one else was around.

She tried to reach
the bread and honey
and the oats
and the milk
and the apples.

She tried this way...
and that way...
but Willa couldn't reach.

Back she went upstairs.

"Willoughby," she called. "Are you awake?"

"I am now," said Willoughby.

"I'm hungry," said Willa.

"Then go and get something to eat."

"I can't reach," said Willa. "Will you come and reach for me?"

Willoughby sighed. "OK. Pass me my slippers."

Paw-in-paw, Willoughby
and Willa went downstairs.
"You can reach because
you are big," said Willa.
"That's right," said Willoughby.
"And one day you'll be big too."
"Will I?" said Willa.

Then they both settled down
to eat breakfast.

"How big will I be?"
asked Willa.

"Oh, very big,"
said Willoughby.

"Will I be bigger than you?"
asked Willa.

"No," said Willoughby.

"Why?" asked
Willa.

"Because I got started
first," said Willoughby.

"And I'll go on getting
bigger too."

"That means you can
wash the dishes," said Willa.

"Sort of," said Willoughby.

"Tell me what it's like to be big," said Willa.

"You can do lots of things," said Willoughby.

"What things?"

"You'll be able to reach the lamp by yourself when you're big," said Willoughby.

"Will I?" said Willa.

"Oh yes," said Willoughby. "And when you're really big, nearly as big as I'll be, you might be able to reach the moon in a rocket!"

"What else will I do when I'm big?" asked Willa.

"You'll be able to stand in
the shower like me and turn
it on by yourself," said Willoughby.
"Will I?" said Willa.
"You'll be able to reach for a towel and
get dried by yourself," said Willoughby.
"Will I?" said Willa.
"And you'll be able to brush your own teeth
without any help," said Willoughby.
"And will Spotty Ted brush his?" asked Willa.
"He hasn't got any teeth," said Willoughby.

"And will I have to make my own bed?"
asked Willa. "Will I have to tidy my own toys?"
"You won't have any toys," said Willoughby.
"You'll be too big for toys."

"Willoughby," said Willa.
"What is it?" said Willoughby.
"I don't ever want to be big."
        "Why not?" said Willoughby.
            "I always want my toys,"
            said Willa.
            "I always want mine too,"
            said Willoughby. "But we
            won't mind, you see. We'll
            have grown-up things
            instead."

"But then I might have to do grown-up things," said Willa.

"Like what?" asked Willoughby.

"Like go out of the door all by myself... like walk down the road all by myself... like be in the world all by myself. There might be nobody there!"

"Spotty Ted will be there," said Willoughby. "You can keep him forever if you like."

"But I might not fit into my chicken slippers any more," said Willa.

"Then you could have some rooster slippers like mine, or some pom-pom slippers like Mum's," said Willoughby. "I know. Let's go and see if Mum's awake."

She wasn't, but they climbed in beside her anyway.

"This is very early morning," she yawned, looking at the clock. "Why don't we just snuggle up for a while?"

"Mum," said Willa. "Were you ever small?"

"I was," said Mum. "Smaller even than you."

"And was I small too?" asked Willoughby.

"To me, you still are," said Mum.

"Tell us, Mum," said Willoughby.

"Tell us what you did
when you were small."

"Well, if I woke up too
early in the morning,
I went back to sleep,"
said Mum.

"Why don't we do that?"

And they did.